THE KNIGHT OF SILK AND STEEL

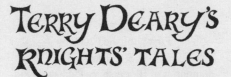

TERRY DEARY'S KNIGHTS' TALES

THE KNIGHT OF SILK AND STEEL

Illustrated by Helen Flook

A & C Black • London

First published 2009 by
A & C Black
an imprint of Bloomsbury Publishing Plc
50 Bedford Square, London WC1B 3DP

www.bloomsbury.com

Text copyright © 2009 Terry Deary
Illustrations copyright © 2009 Helen Flook

The rights of Terry Deary and Helen Flook to be identified as the
author and illustrator of this work have been asserted by them in
accordance with the Copyrights, Designs and Patents Act 1988.

ISBN 978-1-4081-0619-8

A CIP catalogue for this book is available from the British Library.

This book is produced using paper that is made from wood grown in
managed, sustainable forests. It is natural, renewable and recyclable.
The logging and manufacturing processes conform to the
environmental regulations of the country of origin.

Printed and Bound by CPI Group (UK) Ltd, Croydon CR0 4YY

3 5 7 9 10 8 6 4 2

Chapter One
Sword
and Stew

A village in Germany, 1227

The dress was made of finest silk, but now it was faded and worn.

The dress was green with threads of gold, but the threads were broken and torn.

The dress reached down to the muddy road and the edge was tattered and splattered with mud.

The knight rode up to the tavern as the sun was setting and the sky was the colour of blood.

He handed his grey horse to the
groom to feed and water it. The
horse snorted softly as it smelled
the oats and the hay.

The knight pulled his sword
straight and walked to the door of
the tavern. He pushed it open and
looked into the gloomy room.

The room was a pit of filth from the straw on the floor to the ale that swam over the dirty wooden tables.

Some men supped from cups and others chewed on stew in wooden bowls. Some played board games and argued about their game – some just sat on their stools and argued because they wanted to argue.

Dogs wandered round and begged for scraps of stew but found the mutton too tough for their yellow teeth. (The sheep that was in the stew had died of old age.)

Leonard the landlord and his daughter Meg poured the ale from jugs and kept the fire and the candles burning, they slopped the stew and gathered up the empty plates and cups.

Meg was crop-haired, like a boy, and wore trousers when she worked in the tavern.

She saw the door swing open, letting in the dim, red light of dusk. She saw the knight. Her mouth fell open. She gave a scream.

The crowd fell silent. Fifty pairs of eyes were turned towards the door.

Meg tried to speak, but couldn't find her voice.

Sam the blacksmith had a voice and spluttered, "Mmmmf-mmmmf-mm-mm-mmmmf!" (His mouth was full of chewy stew, of course, but everyone in the tavern knew what he meant.)

"Just look at *him*!" Meg gasped at last.

John the gong-farmer sniggered.

Richard the rabbit-catcher giggled.
Simon the snaggle-bodger snorted.

Soon the whole room was
laughing and pointing, pointing and
laughing, slapping the tables, their
legs, their backs, rubbing their eyes
and rolling on their stools. (Helen
the harpist fell off her stool, but that
could have been the ale.)

At last the laughter died away.

"Good evening,
ladies and gentlemen,"
the knight said in
a voice as soft as
fox fur.

"Ooooh!
Ladies!" Tom the
village fool mocked.
"He's talking about
you, Helen!"

Helen the harpist
looked up from
the floor.

"And gentlemen,
he said. That's
you, Tom Fool!"

The man at the door smiled
gently. "I am Ulrich of Bavaria,"
he said, "and I am a knight."

"Yes, but what are you doing here?" Ben the badger-baiter cried.

"I am seeking a room for the night," said Ulrich.

"A knight's night sleep?" Tom Fool asked.

The crowd laughed.

"And a fight," Ulrich said, patting the huge steel sword that hung at his side.

The crowd went suddenly silent (except for Helen the harpist, who snored on the floor). Even the dogs went quiet and stopped chewing on the mutton that was tough as old leather.

No one wanted to fight with a madman.

At last the landlord's daughter, Meg, stepped forward. "We can offer you a room, sir, and some of our fine food!"

Sam the blacksmith, who was still chewing, said what he thought of the fine food. "Mmmmf-mmmmf-mm-mm-mmmmf!"

Ulrich bowed to Meg and thanked her.

"But, sir," said Meg. "I wonder if you could tell us all..."

"Yes?" said Ulrich.

"Why... Why are you wearing a green, silk dress and a long, blond wig?"

Chapter Two
Goats
and Greed

"It is a simple tale," Ulrich said, and he walked towards the bar of the tavern.

Leonard the landlord backed away. The shining steel of the swinging sword filled him with fear.

His daughter Meg was not afraid. "We love tales in this tavern," she said. "But we hear the same ones time and time again. If you have a new tale, then tell us, please!"

Ulrich leaned against the bar.

"I've travelled twenty leagues today. I need a little food and wine to wash the dust from out of my throat."

Leonard the landlord bowed so low he almost scraped the floor. "Of course, my lord, we serve the very finest wine ... for those who can afford to pay!"

The knight lifted a purse that hung from the silken belt around his dress. "I've money ... gold or silver, groats or guilders," he said.

"A groat will buy you wine, and two will buy a plate of stew," Meg said merrily.

"That's *two* groats for our finest wine and *four* groats for our better stew," her father put in greedily.

Ulrich threw a piece of gold upon the counter top. "That should do to buy a drink for everyone here in the tavern... Keep the change," he shrugged, as Leonard the landlord snatched the coin. "When all my new friends have been served, then I shall tell my tale."

Ale splashed into cups, and from the cups slopped into mouths, while Ulrich drained the tavern's finest flagon of rich, red wine.

Meg made sure the man had only plates of lean beef stew and crusty white bread to mop the tasty gravy. The dogs looked up and dribbled down their chops to smell the meal that Meg had made.

At last, the tavern settled back
onto their stools and looked towards
the bar.

Ulrich was a handsome knight.
He wiped his yellow beard carefully
and looked around, and fifty pairs
of eyes looked back. (Well, fifty-five,
if we add in the dogs.)

"My name is Ulrich," he began.
"My tale goes back to when I was
a boy of twelve."

"I'm twelve," Meg said with a grin, and Ulrich nodded.

"I was a squire."

"I know what that is!" said Meg. "It's a boy who helps a knight – he fastens on his armour, cares for his horse and polishes his weapons."

Ulrich nodded once again, then went on with his tale. "My master was a lord of Alsace on the borders of France. Now, knights must have some deeds to do."

"Kill dragons!" Tom Fool said, but Ulrich shook his head.

"I've never seen a dragon, and I think they just exist in old stories told to frighten children. *Real* knights fight for what is right against the greatest evil of them all – wicked men!"

"Ahhhh!" the crowd inside the tavern sighed.

"But there is one fight greater than all other fights," the young knight said. "There is one thing that a knight may swear to live and die for…"

"I know!" Meg squealed. "Yes, I know just what you're going to say."

"A knight should find a lady fair that he can give his life to," Ulrich said.

"A lady *fair*!" Meg moaned. "My hair's as dark as coal."

Ulrich laughed. "When I say fair, I mean fair of face – or pretty.

She doesn't have to have fair hair!"
he said, and pointed to his own
blond wig.

"That's good," said the girl. "Carry
on. When you were twelve..."

"When I was twelve, I first met
with that old man ... Death."

The crowd let out a sorry moan.

Chapter Three
Wine
and Wig

"When I was twelve, my master fell in love with Isabel, the fairest lady in the whole of Austria."

"Then he married her," Sam the blacksmith groaned. "And they lived happy ever after. Pah! We've heard that tale a hundred times. We want the other tale – the one that tells us why you're wearing a green, silk dress!"

"Oh, silence, Sam!" came Helen's voice from somewhere underneath the table. "Let the knight tell us his tale in his own time."

"The Lady Isabel is married," Ulrich went on. "Her husband is a miserable man. He punishes his peasants, uses them as slaves, he's mean with money ... he lets fair Isabel dress in wool instead of silk.

"He holds no feasts and keeps no jesters, guests get dry bread, wine like vinegar and beds that have more fleas than fleece."

"We know his sort," said Ben the badger-baiter quietly. "Your master fought this wicked lord and killed him as dead as some duck's toenail?"

"Oh, no, my story has a much sadder ending," young Ulrich moaned, and sipped his rich, red wine. "My master went off to a joust – a mighty show of knights. Each knight takes it in turn to charge another knight with his lance. The knight who breaks the tip off his lance is the winner. He goes on to fight again and again till there is just one knight left ... the champion."

"Your master fought to be the champion and win his lady's heart?" Meg asked.

"He fought," young Ulrich sighed.
"And lost?"

"And worse. A knight from France
smashed his lance against my
master's shield. The broken splints
of lance went through the eyepiece
of his helmet, through his eye and
clean into his brain!"

"I bet that hurt," Richard the rabbit-catcher gasped.

Helen the harpist sat up straight. "Don't be a fool!" she cried. "It wouldn't hurt at all, for it would kill him dead!"

"It did," said Ulrich. "Such a mess." He supped his wine, as red as dead knight's blood. "I took his armour and vowed that I'd fight on. I'd win the lady's love, I'd fight a hundred knights – five hundred if I must."

"All very well," old John the gong-
farmer said. "So you set off around
the world to fight five hundred
knights. There is a name for knights
like that ... I can't
remember
what it is..."

"Knight errant is the name I think
you want," Simon the snaggle-
bodger smiled (so pleased to show
how much he knew).

"Knight *errant* if you like," old
John went on. "But still you have
to tell us why you wear the dress!"

Ulrich nodded. "The Lady Isabel
is married, so I cannot name her as
my love. Instead, I fight for Venus,
she's the mighty goddess of all love.
I fight for Venus and, to make it
plain, I *dress* as Venus! Venus wig
and Venus dress," he said.

"And Venus beard?" Meg put in.

"No, I set off from Venice at least two years ago. And when you travel on the dusty roads it's hard to find a village with a barber who can give a shave. Some larger towns from time to time."

"Ah ha!" the crowd smiled. This was starting to make sense.

"So, here you are," the landlord said. "You'll stop the night?"

"I will."

"And then you'll travel on again."

The young knight spread his rein-stained hands and said, "I'd like a fight!" He drew his sword. The crowd stepped back. "Oh, not with you, my friends. I meant I want to find a knight to fight. The lord, perhaps, that owns this land?"

Chaper Four
Breakfast and
Butler

"Oooo-arrrrgh!" cried Simon the snaggle-bodger. "What you want's Lord Edmund up at Seckau Castle. He's your man, yes, he's your man."

"The Red Knight's what they call him," Helen the harpist laughed, then lay back on the floor.

"Red Knight, eh? Because he is a warrior, bold and mighty, dressed in armour scarlet red?"

"Nah!" sneered Tom Fool cruelly. "His old armour's red with rust."

Ulrich reached inside his dress and pulled out some parchment. "Here's a challenge to your lord. Take this to him. Tell him I'll meet him in the fields outside the castle after he has dined tomorrow noon."

"I'll take that!" Simon the snagglebodger said. He hurried through the door into the falling night. He whistled through the woods and haunting owls hooted back.

"I'm scared of bears!" poor Simon cried. "I must be mad to walk the woods on such a night."

But he soon saw the castle on the hill and flaming torches lit the gate. The guards were sleeping sloppily, the way they always did.

Simon simply walked right past and hurried up into the hall.

The lord of Seckau sat back, fat and full after his feast. "Ha! Simon! What do you want, lad?" he cried.

"A challenge, lord, from some young knight," the snaggle-bodger said, and waved the piece of parchment.

"Oh, I love a good fight!" Old Lord Seckau smiled and rubbed his hands with joy.

He called a skinny, white-haired servant dressed in black to stand beside his chair.

"Now, Charles, you'll need to work all night. I want my armour shining bright by morning, do you hear?"

"Huh, my lord, you don't want much. There's years of dust and rust to shift, and straps that snapped last time you fought. You do give me the rotten jobs!" the servant whined.

"I pay you well in wine and food and clothes and blankets for your bed, so stop your moaning, Charles. Do the job and wake me in the morning."

Charles raised his nose, and sniffed with hurt, but really it was all a game. By the time the cockerel crowed, the armour shone as bright as any silver moon.

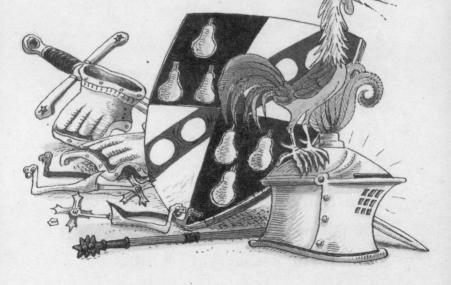

His lordship had a little breakfast
– seven eggs, and six beef pasties,
five large wine cups, four sweet
tartlets, three small cheeses, two
roast chickens and a loaf of bread.

"Fetch my horse, my good man
Charles!" he called.

The man in black raised his fine chin in the air and said, "May I remind you, I'm your butler, *not* your groom. That's the job for the stable lads."

Old Lord Seckau gave a mighty laugh and wrapped an iron hand around the shoulder of the servant. "Charles, my man, you *are* the groom!"

"Since when?"

"Since you *sacked* the stable lads and pocketed their wages. Now, help me fasten on the armour, then go down and saddle my charger. What I need is a little practice. After all, you wouldn't want your lord to lose!"

"Fah!" the servant spat. "I wouldn't mind."

"Oh, yes, you would," his master told him. "This knight Ulrich fights for trophies. If I win, I get a gold ring.  If I lose, then *I* pay him. But see, my dear old servant... *If* I lose, then I will take the money from the wages that *you're* given to pay the grooms!"

"The what?"

"The money that you get to pay the grooms ... the money that you pay yourself, you black-hearted butler. So I lose nothing, you lose all!"

Charles went wobbly at the knees, then pulled himself up straight. "My dear, good Lord, of course you'll win! You always did ... when you were thin and fit and strong. I'll saddle your horse then come and help you climb aboard. The crane is ready in the castle yard!"

Chapter Five
Chargers
and Cheers

Dawn broke over the village tavern
and everyone was wide awake. The
tavern groom was brushing Ulrich's
fine, grey horse until it glowed
bright in the sun.

Leonard the landlord fed the
young knight fresh-baked bread and
honeyed ham, then Ulrich washed
in pure, clear water from the stream.

In the stable, young Meg took
the saddlebags and laid out all the
armour. "I can be your squire," she
told the knight. "Fasten up your
armour, lead your horse and pick
you up when you're knocked down!"

Ulrich nodded. "So you shall be. Venus would be pleased to see a girl who helps us fight her battle! Dust my armour while I put a stitch in this small tear I ripped in my dress!"

Meg was singing as she dusted. Ulrich was happy as he breathed in the morning's good, crisp air. "This is what a knight errant lives for. Fighting for his lady fair."

Ulrich pushed a wandering pig away then tucked his sewing kit into a saddlebag. With Meg's help, he strapped himself into his armour and slipped the dress on top.

The whole village gathered round and made a line along the road.

Ulrich clanged and clattered as he
walked up the path to the hill. A line
of cheery village people followed,
work forgotten.

Charles had placed a row of fences made from brushwood in a line across the field. Old Lord Seckau would ride down one side, Ulrich's Venus down the other. When they neared, they'd lower their lances and each would try to smash the lance tip on his rival's chest. If it was a strong, true hit then one knight could be smashed clean from his saddle.

Ulrich mounted on his charger, and young Meg passed up his helmet. Seckau waited at the far end and waved a cheery, metal glove.

Charles the butler held a white rag.
"When I drop the flag, you ride.
God bless you! God bless us all!"

Each knight lowered the eye guard
on his helmet, each squire passed
his lord a lance. Fifty village people
held their breath and even birds fell
silent in the sky.

Charles the butler dropped the
flag.

Old Lord Seckau moved his heels and dug sharp spurs into his horse's side. The horse went *snicker*, gave a snort and moved at a gentle trot. (Well, it was old and his master weighed him down like castle stone.)

Ulrich spurred his fine, grey charger. The beast rose up on its hind legs and pawed the air like a dancing bear.

Then it lowered its head and struck the ground with hooves of thunder.

Off it sped towards Lord Seckau, faster than a speeding hare. Ulrich raced a hundred paces while Lord Seckau plodded ten.

The village cheered him, grass and clods of earth and worms flew up as he charged on while Lord Seckau plodded forth.

Lord Seckau brought his heavy lance down and took aim at Ulrich.

They were fifty paces apart.

Ulrich lowered his lance and tried to take aim at Lord Seckau, but it's hard to aim when you're galloping fast.

Forty paces, and Lord Seckau plodded almost to a stop.

Thirty paces, Ulrich's lance tip wobbled.

Twenty paces, Lord Seckau stopped and let his enemy race towards his waiting lance.

Ten paces, blond hair flew from underneath the helmet, green-gold silk dress billowed in the wind. Venus was a glorious sight riding for fair lady's love.

Three paces, Lord Seckau's lance tip crunched into the breastplate of

fair Venus. Ulrich's lance tip pointed
to the noonday sun. He'd missed ...
with worse shame to come.

Chapter Six
Lances and
Legends

Old Lord Seckau sat there like a castle wall and did not move. As speeding Ulrich hurried past, the lance smashed him from his saddle. Ulrich tumbled backwards, skirt flying over his helmeted head.

Lord Seckau laughed.

Ulrich hit the green turf with a clatter that shook starlings from the trees a mile away.

Meg sobbed and ran across the grass towards the fallen man.

She pulled the helmet from his head
and threw the wig aside.

"My lord," she moaned.
"He's killed you dead!"

"I don't think so," Ulrich
whispered and gave a little gasp
for air. "Just help me to my feet,
my faithful squire."

The girl and Leonard the landlord dragged him up as Charles the butler helped Lord Seckau down.

The old lord grinned a red-faced grin and walked towards the unhurt Ulrich. "You young men are all the same," he said. "In too much haste. You need to learn that in a charge, swift deer don't beat a standing bull."

Ulrich smiled. "I'll learn, good lord." He reached into the leather purse that hung from his silken belt. "The payment for my lesson's one gold ring," he said, and passed the prize across.

The knights removed their iron gloves and shook each other's hand.

Someone caught the great, grey horse and led the way back down the hill.

Meg sighed. "You'll never win your lady fair if you don't fight more carefully."

Ulrich nodded. "Oh, I win as many as I lose. What matters is I play the game. I do my best and no one can do more. I'm not like all the other knights – the ones who stay at home and use their strength to beat and bully poor peasants."

They reached the tavern. Meg helped Ulrich take off his armour and pack it safely away.

"Can I come with you, Ulrich? Be your squire?" the crop-haired girl asked quietly.

The knight faced the sun that sparkled in the gold threads of his shabby dress.

"No, Meg, the greatest knights always ride alone. Go home," he smiled. "You'll have your own hard battles to fight, for life is often cruel." Then he climbed onto his horse and turned its head towards the west.

"I'll not forget you, or the lesson that I learned," Meg shouted after him. "I'll do my best and no one can do more."

The knight rode away from
the tavern as the sun was setting
and turned the sky to the colour
of blood.

Epilogue

Ulrich of Liechtenstein was born in Austria in 1200. He fell in love with his master's lady (he says) when he was just twelve years old. He then travelled around Europe as a knight errant to prove his love by fighting anyone.

He set off on a journey from Venice to Vienna, and called his travels "The Venus Tour" because Venus is the goddess of love. He dressed in a long, blond wig and a woman's dress so he looked like Venus ... Venus with a beard. That was enough to put any enemy off!

Ulrich must have been very rich because he owned three castles and was able to offer a gold ring to anyone who could defeat him. Anyone who he beat had to give a gift to his lady and bow to the four corners of the Earth.

Ulrich said he broke 307 lances and won just as many fights. But he was not that great a warrior. He had to give away 271 rings, so he lost almost as many fights as he won.

We know about him because he wrote a long story-poem about his adventures and called his poem "Service of the Lady".

When Ulrich finished the Venus Tour, he rode to his lady's

castle. But what did she say? "Go off and do it again!" And when he had fought even more battles for her, did she fall in love with him? Sorry. No, she didn't. She was a hard lady to please.

The odd thing about knights was they liked to fight for a married woman ... a woman they could never win. Ulrich was disgusted with other knights of the time. He thought they were not true men. He wanted to show them how a real knight lived and fought ... even if he had to wear a dress to prove it.

Ulrich went on to be a great lord in Austria ... even with a broken heart. He died at the good old age of 78.

TERRY DEARY'S
GREEK TALES

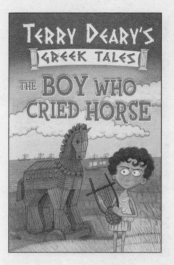

TERRY DEARY'S
GREEK TALES
THE **BOY WHO CRIED HORSE**

TERRY DEARY'S
GREEK TALES
THE **TORTOISE** AND THE **DARE**

TERRY DEARY'S
GREEK TALES
THE **LION'S SLAVE**

TERRY DEARY'S
GREEK TALES
THE **TOWN MOUSE** AND THE **SPARTAN HOUSE**

TERRY DEARY'S ROMAN TALES

THE GOOSE GUARDS

THE CAPTIVE CELT

THE FATAL FIRE

THE GRIM GHOST